North America

AMERICAN ALLIGATORS

by Tyler Omoth

FOCUS READERS

North Star
EDITIONS

www.northstareditions.com

Produced for North Star Editions by Red Line Editorial.

Photographs ©: Heiko Kiera/Shutterstock Images, cover, 1; Juan Gracia/ Shutterstock Images, 4–5; stephenallen75/iStockphoto, 8–9; Arto Hakola/ Shutterstock Images, 11; Svetlana Foote/Shutterstock Images, 13, 29; TonyTaylorStock/iStockphoto, 14–15; John Zocco/Shutterstock Images, 16; Catcher of Light, Inc./Shutterstock Images, 18; &#169 red_moon_rise/ iStockphoto, 21; wowwa/iStockphoto, 22–23, 27 (top); David Unger/Shutterstock Images, 25, 27 (bottom right); KlemannLee/Shutterstock Images, 26; Brian Lasenby/Shutterstock Images, 27 (bottom left)

ISBN
978-1-63517-027-6 (hardcover)
978-1-63517-083-2 (paperback)
978-1-63517-186-0 (ebook pdf)
978-1-63517-136-5 (hosted ebook)

Library of Congress Control Number: 2016951027

Printed in the United States of America
Mankato, MN
November, 2016

About the Author

Tyler Omoth is the author of more than two dozen books for children on topics ranging from baseball to Stonehenge to turkey hunting. He loves going to sporting events and taking in the sun at the beach. Omoth lives in sunny Brandon, Florida, with his wife, Mary.

TABLE OF CONTENTS

CHAPTER 1

FRESHWATER REPTILES

The American alligator is the largest **reptile** in North America. The greatest numbers of these **predators** live in Florida, southern Georgia, and Louisiana.

The largest American alligators are approximately 11 feet (3.4 m) long.

Pacific
Ocean

North
America

Atlantic
Ocean

where American
alligators live

American alligators live in the southeastern
corner of the United States.

Alligators thrive in freshwater.

They spend their time in swamps,

rivers, streams, and lakes.

Alligators often dig out **dens**

in the **banks** of the water. This is

where they rest.

Alligators sometimes dig pits in shallow waters. These are called gator holes. During the winter months, less rain falls. The gator holes collect water. This allows the alligators to survive until the weather changes and rain brings more water.

FUN FACT

Unlike most animals, alligators have changed very little on Earth for millions of years. Some scientists call them living fossils.

CHAPTER 2

SCALY SWIMMERS

Alligators have short legs and are low to the ground. **Scales** cover their long bodies. Their backs have rows of bony plates. Alligators are usually either greenish-brown or black.

Alligators' coloring makes it easy for them to hide both in murky water and on grassy banks.

An alligator's head is long and rounded. Even with its jaws closed, many sharp teeth stick out. An alligator's jaws help it catch **prey.** The muscles that hold the jaws shut are very strong. Once the alligator clamps down its jaws, prey cannot escape.

FUN FACT

An alligator continually loses old teeth and grows new ones. One alligator may have as many as 3,000 teeth during its lifetime.

**Alligators use their strong jaws
to catch and hold prey.**

An alligator uses its long and powerful tail to swim. It also uses its tail as a weapon. Sometimes alligators attack one another. To fight back, an alligator swings its heavy tail with great force. The tail smacks the other alligator.

Alligators get around in water very well. They have webbed feet

FUN FACT

An alligator can use its tail to swim more than 20 miles per hour (32 km/h).

PARTS OF AN AMERICAN ALLIGATOR

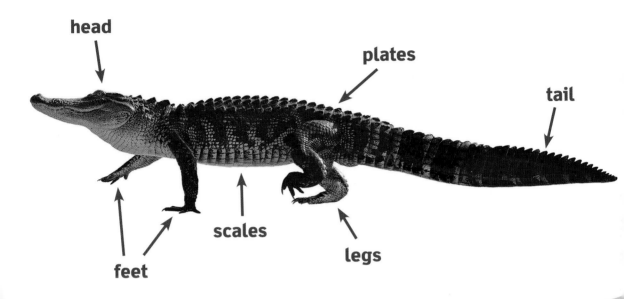

head

plates

tail

scales

feet

legs

that help them swim fast. Yet they are slow on land. They can lunge quickly for a short distance, but they are not fast across long distances.

CHAPTER 3

SENSING AND STALKING PREY

Alligators have very good eyesight, hearing, and smell. This makes them excellent hunters. When an alligator sees a target, it slowly **stalks** it.

An alligator lunges into water after prey.

Alligators use their powerful legs and tail to jump vertically out of the water.

Alligators stalk both in the water and on land. The alligator gets as close as possible to its prey. Then it lunges with great power. The alligator clamps its jaws down to snatch its meal.

Young alligators are very small. They survive by eating mostly insects, spiders, and worms. As young alligators grow, they start to eat small fish and frogs.

Adult alligators eat mostly fish, birds, and other small animals.

Fish, birds, and other small animals that
live in or near water are easy targets for
alligators.

Any animal that comes to the water to drink could end up as an alligator's meal. Alligators will even attack and eat larger creatures, such as deer and cows.

FUN FACT

Alligators are one of the very few animals that can live to be 50 years old in the wild.

EXTRAORDINARY EYELIDS

An alligator's extraordinary senses, physical build, and eyelids make it a top predator. The eyes, nostrils, and ears are all on the very top of the alligator's head. This way the alligator can see, smell, and hear prey while hidden almost entirely underwater.

The eyelids come in handy when the alligator does go underwater. Alligators have two sets of eyelids. The outer set matches the alligator's skin. This set closes from top to bottom. The second set is underneath the outer set. These eyelids

Alligators close their pupils to small slits in bright sunlight.

close from side to side. They are crystal clear. They serve as goggles so the alligator can see prey underwater.

CHAPTER 4

ALLIGATOR FAMILIES

Alligators are mostly **solitary** animals. But they do come together each spring to mate. After mating, the female alligator builds a nest. She clears an area and creates a small bowl in the earth.

> **Baby alligators hatch from their eggs.**

She brings sticks, leaves, and mud to the area. She packs everything down until the nest is complete. Then she lays as many as 60 eggs. She covers them with more sticks, leaves, and mud.

After approximately two months, the eggs hatch. The young alligators are called hatchlings.

FUN FACT

Hatchlings are only 6 to 8 inches (15 to 20 cm) long when they hatch.

Instead of being a single color, hatchlings are black with yellow stripes. This coloring helps them hide.

They start to grunt. This sound calls the mother back to the nest. She carefully uncovers the nest to let out the new hatchlings.

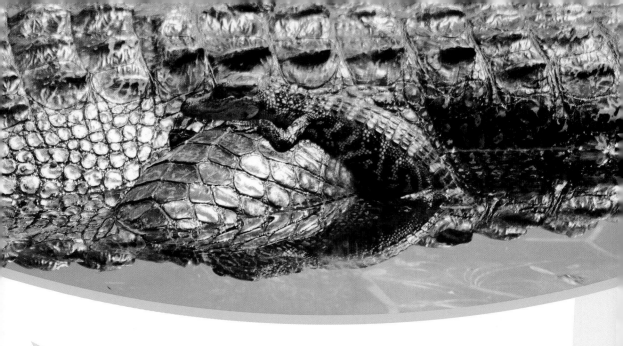

Young alligators stay very close to their mothers.

The young alligators are vulnerable to predators. The mother protects her young. She attacks anything that gets too close to them. After two to three years, the young alligators are large enough to protect themselves.

AMERICAN ALLIGATOR
LIFE CYCLE

Hatchlings hatch after approximately two months in the eggs.

Young alligators stay near their mothers.

When they are approximately two to three years old, alligators live alone.

AMERICAN ALLIGATORS

Write your answers on a separate piece of paper.

1. What do you think you were supposed to learn from reading this book?

2. Would you want to live near American alligators? Why or why not? If you do live near them, have you seen one?

3. In which corner of the United States do American alligators live?
   - A. southeastern
   - B. southwestern
   - C. northeastern

4. Why do you think American alligators are slower on land than they are in water?
   - A. They have long tails.
   - B. They have short legs.
   - C. They have scales.

5. What does **lunges** mean in this book?

    A. has a lot of strength

    B. leaps or plunges forward suddenly

    C. crawls very close to something

The alligator gets as close as possible to its prey. Then it **lunges** with great power.

6. What does **vulnerable** mean in this book?

    A. comfortable with

    B. near or close to

    C. easily damaged

The young alligators are **vulnerable** to predators. The mother protects her young.

Answer key on page 32.

GLOSSARY

banks
The parts of sloping land along the sides of a river.

dens
The homes of wild animals.

predators
Animals that kill and eat other animals.

prey
An animal that is hunted and eaten by a different animal.

reptile
A cold-blooded animal that slithers or crawls on short legs.

scales
The thin, flat, overlapping pieces of hard skin that cover the bodies of fish and reptiles.

solitary
Alone or without company.

stalks
Hunts or follows something quietly.

TO LEARN MORE

BOOKS

Herrington, Lisa M. *Crocodiles and Alligators.* New York: Scholastic, 2015.

Hirsch, Rebecca E. *American Alligators: Armored Roaring Reptiles.* Minneapolis: Lerner Publications, 2015.

Marsh, Laura. *National Geographic Readers: Alligators and Crocodiles.* Washington, DC: National Geographic, 2015.

NOTE TO EDUCATORS

Visit **www.focusreaders.com** to find lesson plans, activities, links, and other resources related to this title.

INDEX

D
dens, 6

F
feet, 12

G
gator holes, 7

H
hatchlings, 24, 25, 27

J
jaws, 10, 17

N
nest, 23, 24, 25

P
prey, 10, 17, 20–21

S
scales, 9
senses, 20

T
tail, 12

Answer Key: 1. Answers will vary; **2.** Answers will vary; **3.** A; **4.** B; **5.** B; **6.** C